Maurice Jones

I'm Going On A DRAGON HUNT

Pictures by Charlotte Firmin

PUFFIN BOOKS

Hallo, what's this?

It's tall grass.

Can't walk round it.

Can't leap over it.

Have to charge through it.

Hallo, what's this?

It's a wide river.

Can't swim under it.

Can't float on top of it.

Have to sail across it.

Hallo, what's this?

It's a tall tree.

Can't jump over it.

Can't chop through it.

Think I'll climb up to the top.

Can't fly over it.

Can't jump across it.

Have to swing to the other side.

Hallo,
what's this?

It's thick mud.

Can't tunnel under it.

Can't drive across it.

Have to squelch through it.

Hallo, what's this?

It's a cave.

Think I'll take a look inside.

Feels like the tail of a...

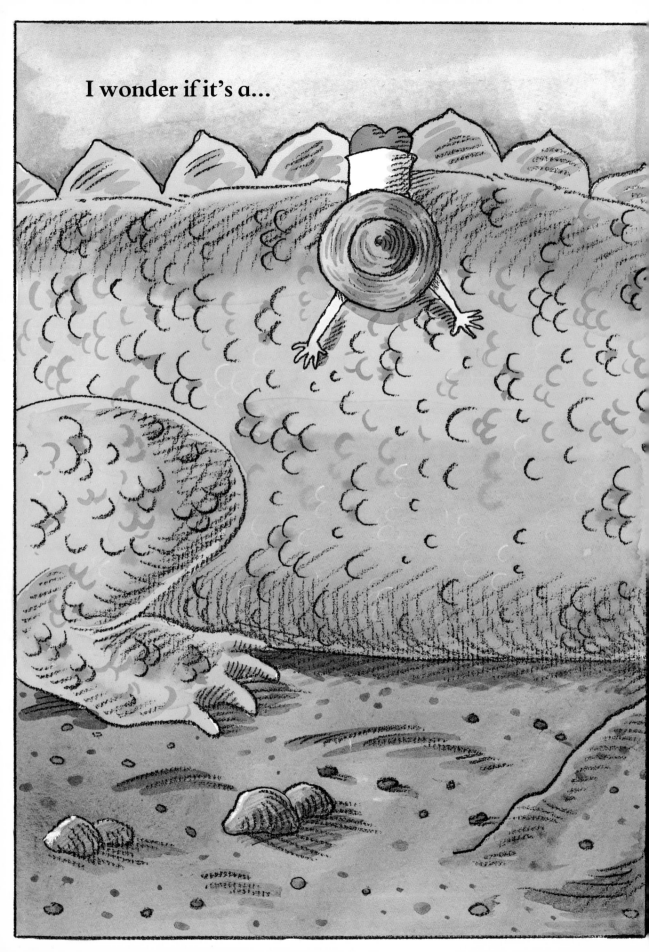

I'll just look round this corner...

Oh no, it's a dragon!

I'm not staying here!

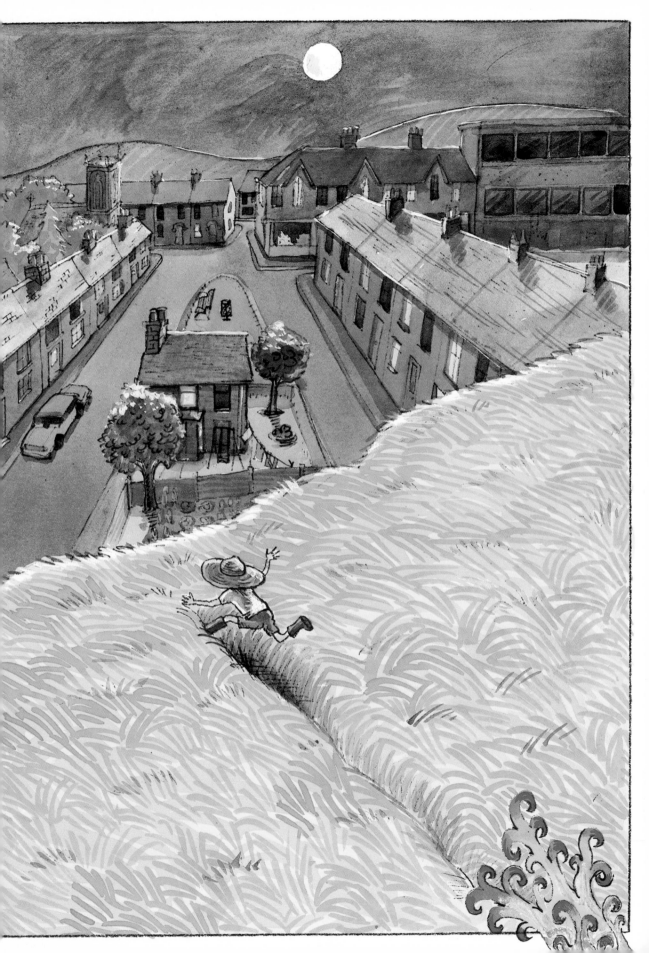

Phew! Safe at last.